THE

HAUNTED BOOKSHELF

he telling or reading of ghost stories during long, dark, and cold Christmas nights is a yuletide ritual dating back to at least the eighteenth century, and was once as much a part of Christmas tradition as decorating fir trees, feasting on goose, and the singing of carols. During the Victorian era many magazines printed ghost stories specifically for the Christmas season. These "winter tales" didn't necessarily explore Christmas themes. Rather, they were offered as an eerie pleasure to be enjoyed on Christmas Eve with the family, adding a supernatural shiver to the seasonal chill.

The tradition remained strong in the British Isles (and her colonies) throughout much of the twentieth century, though in recent years it has been on the wane. Certainly, few people in Canada or the United States seem to know about it any longer. This series of small books seeks to rectify this, to revive a charming custom for the long, dark nights we all know so well here at Christmastime.

THE HAUNTED BOOKSHELF

THE HAUNTED BOOKSHELF

A ROOM IN A RECTORY

A ROOM IN A RECTORY

ANDREW CALDECOTT

A GHOST STORY FOR CHRISTMAS

DESIGNED & DECORATED BY SETH

BIBLIOASIS

ARROW IN BOUNDS, but wide in variety, the garden of Tilchington Rectory was one of the most beautiful in the South Country. It lay in a hollow, some four to five chains broad, down the middle of which ran a small and clear brook marked on the ordnance map as R. Tilch, but beloved of its riparians as, simply, our stream. For half of its course through the Rectory grounds the little river was impounded by successive dams to form three pools. The two upper of these provided easy watering for vegetables, while the third—into which a waterfall splashed between two clumps of bamboo under overhanging fronds of *Osmunda* fern—was the central and distinctive feature of the flower garden. On either side were sloping lawns and to the north of it stood the Rectory house, mainly in the Georgian architecture, but partly Victorianised by plate-glass windows. From the third pool, the stream cascaded down through a rock garden to the level of its natural bed, along which it dimpled and chattered by the side of the gravelled carriage drive, past rose-garden and orchard, until it slipped away from the rectory precincts, over a stone sill set in a small arch beneath the boundary wall. All this description has to be in the past tense, because the Ecclesiastical Commissioners have since sold both parsonage and glebe, and, for all that the writer knows, the fell hand of the improver may have fallen upon house, garden and rivulet.

That future rectors of Tilchington would need to live in humbler and less lovely environment never entered the mind of the present incumbent as, on the 17th June, 1900, from a deck-chair on the further lawn, he gazed across ornamental water and flower beds towards a small shrubbery at the eastern end of the house where he had just finished clipping some too exuberant Portugal laurels. He now surveyed the result of his labour with something of that satisfaction which the author of Genesis ascribes to the Creator, who, looking upon his creation, saw that it was good. The Reverend Nigel Tylethorpe was, and appeared, a fortunate and happy young man of thirty or so: happy in his ancestry, in his inheritance from a lately deceased great-uncle of a comfortable financial competency, in education, in mental endowment, in physical looks, in athletic prowess and (for the living of Tilchington was worth over eight hundred a year) in early ecclesiastical preferment. Nor was his parish less fortunate in him than he in Tilchington. Mr Bugles, sexton and verger, had given words to general opinion when he remarked to the People's Warden at the flower show that "t'new parson be the sort of man as'll do us good without us noticing."

From the shrubbery the Reverend Nigel's eyes passed, with a foreboding of more clipping to be done on the morrow, to the climbers on the house itself. Of these there was a profuse variety: a japonica, wistaria, jasmine, roses and two kinds of ampelopsis. An intrusion into their midst, which he did not admire, was a rectangular patch of thickly-set ivy, which rather ostentatiously concealed a shuttered window on the ground floor. A slight frown flitted across the young man's face, and the pruning shears chattered impatiently in his hand as scissors do in a barber's. He would undoubtedly need to have a final battle with his housekeeper over that silly business of the disused room. Miss Roberta Pristin had served his predecessor for more years than the delicate conventions governing a woman's age would allow her to admit. At his death she had, with persuasive humour, asked Mr Tylethorpe to take her over with the rest of the Rectory fixtures. Except for this one matter of the locked room he did not regret having done so. A bachelor requires quasi-maternal attention, and Miss Pristin was quasi-maternal without being unduly familiar.

The young rector's thoughts were temporarily diverted from this matter of the empty room by the quarter chime of a clock in his dining-room, the french windows of which lay wide open. In another fifteen minutes, at half-past six, he would read the evening office in the chancel of his church, and so he must have a quick wash and brush up after his gardening. The next we see of him, therefore, is five minutes later as he passes across the narrow paddock separating rectory from churchyard. Mention may be found in more than one architectural handbook of the treasures and oddities of St Botolph's, Tilchington: the twelfth-century frescoes, the long tunnel-like hagioscope, the Early English colonnade set on Norman piers and capitals, the narrow chancel arch with remains of screen and rood, etcetera. Nineteenth-century restoration had been unusually discriminative and restrained; so much so that the west end of the building had been left just as it emerged from the demolition of a large and ugly gallery. To regulate the light at the turn of the staircase, now no more, to this gallery a narrow lancet window in the western wall of the south aisle had been walled up and replaced at a higher level by a wood-framed, square-paned window of domestic pattern. The retention by the restorers of a sacred edifice of so secular a feature may have been due to the fact that the glass, though not stained, had received superficial pigmentation and bore a spirited, if unusual, representation of St Michael vanquishing the Prince of Evil.

Mr Tylethorpe resented the survival of a window so completely out of period with the rest of the church and, having read the office and re-hung his surplice in the vestry, he walked down the south aisle with intent to visualise what would be the effect of walling it up and re-opening the lancet window, should the necessary money and faculty be forthcoming. From such general observation, he proceeded to particular examination of the offending feature. There were nine panes, each one foot square, in a main frame of three by three; and the artist had had to dispose his figures accordingly. The top middle pane displayed the haloed head of Michael; the one below it his body; and the nethermost his feet planted firmly upon the prostrate form of Satan, whose proud and rather beautiful head projected from a scaly saurian body. By comparison the visage of the victorious archangel seemed commonplace and slightly bovine. The remaining panes on either side of the central three were taken up with Michael's wings above and with flames emanating from his trampled adversary below. In the two bottom corners, right and left, small oblong frames bore the legends 'Anno 1798' and 'Rev. xii. 7' respectively.

As Mr Tylethorpe glanced at these inscriptions a sudden bright beam from the westering sun flashed through the oblongs and disclosed to his view some very faint writing which a moment before had been invisible. The characters under 'Anno 1798' looked like 'NICOLAS PHAYNE PINXIT', and those under the biblical citation as 'YE TRIUMPH OF AUTHORITIE OVER INTELLIGENCE'. It took the Rector but a moment to realise that they had been imprinted by a die or stamp held upside down; unless, indeed, the writing was intentionally antipodean.

"So it really was him," muttered the Rector ungrammatically as, standing before the carved list of former incumbents on a panel in the porch, he picked out the name of Nicolas Fayne, 1796–1801. From the porch to a tiny triangle of ground between a large yew tree, the south wall of the graveyard and the swing-gate at its south-west corner took but a minute of his homeward walk. Here again on a flat, heavy, horizontal tomb-slab level with the surrounding grass stood out the name of Nicholas Phaine ("Why couldn't he stick to one spelling?" grumbled the Rector); and, beneath it, the words: "Found Dead January 27th MDCCCI." So village tradition had been proved right about that window. Perhaps it might not be far wrong on one or two other points? The triumph of authority over intelligence, indeed! No wonder the inscription was all topsy-turvy: just as well that it had become illegible. Mental derangement was, of course, the most charitable, as it was the most rational, explanation.

The boom of his dinner gong reverberating across the paddock recalled the Rector from speculative reconstructions of parochial history to a pleasantly certain anticipation of the imminent repast. He had a good cook and a good cellar.

2

IN CONVERSATION WITH his housekeeper after breakfast next morning Mr Tylethorpe declared an immediate intention to inspect the vacant room. Remembering previous parleys on this subject he felt some surprise that she expressed neither remonstrance nor apprehension.

"Very well, sir; and, of course, you'll need the key. I always keep it in this drawer; yes, here it be."

On his way down the passage, he examined the wooden tab by which she had handed it to him. On it was neatly cut in capital letters:

SERMON CHAMBER

RE-OPENED 1858

and underneath in his predecessor, Mr Hempstede's, handwriting appeared in faded ink the injunction: "Keep Locked." The key turned readily in the keyhole; for, so long as Miss Pristin had been in charge, the room had been subject to a weekly sweeping. "An empty place'll always get dirt from somewhere," she used to say; "what with rats and all." With no inlet or outlet for ventilation other than the chimney, the Rector had expected the chamber to smell fusty and musty: he was relieved, therefore, to find its air not unduly oppressive, and proceeded to light the candle which he had brought with him for purposes of inspection. Only two thin streaks of daylight penetrated the shuttered and ivied window. The dimensions were commodious enough—some twenty foot square—for the library or study which he so badly required. That all his reading and writing should be done in a dark corner of the dining-room, subject to the many interruptions inseparable from a punctual preparation and removal of meals, was fair neither to himself nor to the congregation that had to listen to discourses composed under such conditions. Carefully pacing the distance between the side walls and the central projection of fireplace and chimney in the southern wall he was gratified to find that his two glazed bookcases would exactly fit the recesses. The ceiling would require re-plastering; the walls, papering; and much of the floor, re-planking. The wainscot was rotten and must be replaced. A modern fireplace and mantelpiece were also desiderata, if he could afford them, as he thought he could. Gently locking the door behind him Mr Tylethorpe manifested his satisfaction with what he had seen by swinging the key wheel-wise by its tab and string as he returned, whistling, down the passage.

"I wonder, Miss Pristin," he remarked as he gave it back to her, "whether you would

tell me all you know about that room. You've hinted at certain things, you know!"

"I can only tell, Sir, as I've already told; nor do I know no more. Him as was took in there, more nor a hundred year ago, is buried up by t' church yew, in that parcel of weeds as was never holied, they say. Nobody cared to bide where he were took, so they bricked up door and window and t' room had no hole to it for nigh sixty year. Then come old parson Witacre and set it open again; but for all he called it his 'sermon chamber' no sermon did parson Witacre ever preach; for he had impeditations in his speech, and had to hire a guinea curate over from Frampton for to read service whenever unavoidable. My dear late master, 'e come next; and how long it was afore he give order to lock up t' room I don't rightly know: but locked it were what time I come to him and ever after. I mind, Sir, one of them early days asking him to let me use it for linen and what not; but 'No,' he says; and 'Why not?' say I. 'Roberta,' he answers, that kind and solemn as were always his way with me, 'It is wiser to learn from precept than by suffering. You leave that room alone.' Them were his words; and leave it alone I ever have, and will; except, of course, for the cleaning which is next to godliness and therefore done regular. That's all I know, Sir, and make of it what you will: but he were a wise and good man, were my late master; and 'Leave it alone,' he says, 'for it be better to learn from precept than by suffering.' Them were his words."

The Rector smiled upon his housekeeper with condescending benevolence: "Thank you very much, Miss Pristin. I do not of course question for a moment Mr Hempstede's decision to keep the apartment locked and in permanent disuse. In such matters each must be governed by his or her conscience and discretion. I myself naturally mislike the idea of associating the performance of any work pertaining to my sacred office with the reputed scene of a mysterious and violent death. I have, however, analysed my distaste and discovered it to be rooted in sentiment rather than reason; and it would be clearly wrong in me to allow sentiment to acquire the appearance, if not indeed the nature, of superstition. I shall, therefore, take immediate steps to have the room restored and redecorated; and, although I shall certainly not allude to it by the name of sermon chamber, I intend to use it for writing my sermons and for reading. I have no doubt that your late master, if he were here with us today—and who shall say that he is not?—would appreciate my reasoning and applaud my decision. And by the way, Miss Pristin, don't forget to serve butter with the baked potatoes."

On his way to the dining-room, the Reverend Nigel's conscience smote him for having been what he could not remember having ever been before: pompous and polysyllabic; quite eighteenth-century, in fact! Arrived at his desk he promptly penned a note to Messrs Burnidge & Hesselton, Builders and Decorators, of Minton Road, Trentchester, asking them to send a representative to advise regarding certain points of interior decoration contemplated by him at Tilchington Rectory. Within ten days the representative had come, inspected, advised, estimated, quoted, and eventually carried away in his pocket what he represented to his employers as "quite a tidy little order."

To the Rector's keen disappointment the repair and refurbishing of the room took no less than three months, although Burnidge & Hesselton's young man had indicated a maximum period of five weeks. There was not merely delay, but delay from unpleasant causes. Language used by the foreman plasterer, however interesting for a certain archaism and singularity, was nevertheless such as Mr Tylethorpe could not let pass without complaint. That the foreman regularly officiated as cross bearer at the ritualistic church of St Terence, Trentchester (although pleaded in extenuation by its scandalised Vicar) seemed insufficiently explanatory of his vocabulary or of its unrestricted use in a country rectory. From this time forward there unhappily came about a distance and a coolness between Father Prodnose and Mr Tylethorpe. The next untoward incident was the infliction of corporal chastisement by the paperhanger on his "holiday apprentice," as he described a very youthful assistant. This in due course brought to Tilchington on investigatory visits an inspector of the Royal Society for Prevention of Cruelty to Children and a minor official of the Paperhangers' Union. All such events wasted time; but what irritated the Rector beyond endurance was Miss Pristin's attitude of obvious unconcern towards what might be going forward, or not going forward, in the room under repair. If only she would quote his predecessor's injunction to "leave the room alone," in reference to the present hindrances, he had his retort—and a very waspish one—ready for her. But she gave him no opening whatever for conversation in the matter, and it became annoyingly clear to him that the effect of Mr Hempstede's words on her simple but strong mind had been to place the room outside her range of thought or observation. It just did not exist for her; and Mr Tylethorpe felt as though he could have tolerated anything more easily than such total disinterest. It was perhaps well for both rector and housekeeper that, in mid-September, the former left for ten days holiday in Scotland, and did not return until the last week of that month when the room had been finished and the workmen gone.

He had left behind him a plan showing the disposition of furniture in his new study, and he was, therefore, able to ensconce himself in it on the very evening of his arrival, as soon as he had taken supper. A roaring fire of Welsh coal provided pleasant contrast to the equinoctially blusterous night without. Its reflection on ceiling, bookcases, armchairs, large writing-table, curtains and pictures suffused a general sense of cosiness and comfort. Mr Tylethorpe was specially pleased with the two pictures, the framing of which had been his last order before leaving for Scotland. They were not his own, but belonged to the church, being the largest of a series of water-colour drawings by an artist member of the Southshire Archaeological Society that had been kept rolled up in the iron chest which protected the parish registers. The one above the fireplace was a reproduction—one thirtieth the size of the original—of the Doom fresco above the chancel arch; while that on the opposite wall was a full-size replica of the picture painted on the square window, already described, in the south aisle. As the firelight alternately flickered and faltered, the face of the nether figure in the latter started into life and, as quickly, relapsed into a flat gloom. Its beauty in the original had not been lost in the copying, but the water-colour artist had introduced into its expression the vestige of a smile; faint, it was true, but sufficient to negative (what the subject so essentially demanded) an appearance of utter defeat and despair in the vanquished. The figure of the archangel, on the other hand, retained all the stolidity of its prototype in the window; and, from where the Rector now viewed the picture, it appeared almost as though St Michael, in the repletion of victory, had allowed his eyes to close in sleep. Mr Tylethorpe felt much inclined to do likewise, for the grouse had been well hung and well cooked and his uncle's port better than any he had drunk on holiday. "Bother you, Mike," he apostrophised the angel, somewhat irreverently; "it's your beastly festival that keeps me from enjoying my armchair: but I simply must finish my Michaelmas sermon."

Refilling his pipe, he sat down at the writing-table to the notes which he had jotted down in the train. "Why, to be sure," he looked again towards the figures on the wall, "I've dealt with only one side of the picture. I must fill in the other." For the next fifteen minutes his pen travelled over the paper rapidly and without pause: then, thrusting his notes into a drawer, he rose to have a look at his books. The older, calf-bound volumes of his uncle's collection made an odd miscellany: for instance, that set of *Annual Registers*, could there be anything still readable in them? He picked out one at random and sank sumptuously into an armchair. "The Year's Poetick Review" looked promising, but the laureate flatulence of Pye quickly disgusted him. Here, however, was something more crisp and terse; and, by Jove, the very thing to round off the end of his sermon! He had read through the lines three times, admiring their relevance to the theme of his discourse, when the book slipped to the floor with a bang. What! Surely he had not fallen asleep? No: obviously not, because he had memorised the verses perfectly and would now write them down. He resumed his seat at the table for that purpose and soon had them on paper. But did the first line of the last verse begin, "So sleep not" or "So be not"? He had better verify. This should have been easy enough, for he had not yet replaced the volume in the bookcase. Three times he went through "The Poetick Review," the third time page by page; but the verses eluded re-discovery. Never mind! He had noted them down with sufficient accuracy for a pulpit quotation, and it was now quite time for bed: no need to be meticulous.

He placed a guard against the grate, turned down the reading-lamp, and, carrying a candle, stayed at the door for a parting look at his new-found cosiness. The fire still glowed, and the room seemed loath for him to go. He quite envied the shadow cast by the fire-screen on the further armchair; it seemed so to enjoy the red leather upholstery. As a coal fell and flared, it appeared indeed to assume a momentary substantiality. "Good night," said the Rector. If he had thought of it, that was the first time he had ever bidden good night to a shadow. But he was not thinking: long railway journeys are so dreadfully tiring.

3

NIGEL TYLETHORPE, THOUGH no orator, was by no means a bad preacher. This was because he took trouble to think of what he was going to say and to give his thoughts a clear and concise expression. Mr Bugles as usual was representative of majority opinion among the congregation when he remarked "as how parson's sermons be well cooked and served up right-like, neither too warm nor too cold." Many of his listeners however felt the peroration of his Michaelmas homily to have an unpleasant temperature: the sort of heat in fact that gives a chill. Having in the earlier stages of this discourse dilated upon the celestial ministry of angels (their service in heaven, errands upon earth, and vigil over mankind), the Rector suddenly changed his tune to a minor key and gave to some of its chords a distinctly ugly modulation. Just as all good was impersonated in the Deity, so was all evil impersonated in the Devil. Analogous to the Former's army of angels were the black cohorts of the latter. People had become accustomed to a comfortable and one-sided belief in guardian angels, but when the average man spoke of his evil genius did he realise that he was naming a companion equally constant and quite as personal? It was necessary that all should face facts; especially elemental facts. To deny or ignore the emissaries of the Evil One was to provoke their attentions. With the eye of the spirit he felt that he could detect unbidden visitants among his congregation at that moment. They were about to sing hymn No. 335. Why the compilers of *Hymns Ancient and Modern* had placed it among their selections "For the Young" he did not know. Perhaps it was because the words presented only one side, of a picture whose other side Age, preferring to pretend blindness thereto itself, must logically hide from the eyes of Youth. Opportunely enough, continued the Rector, he had recently come across in an old book certain verses which would serve to supplement the hymn and enable them to conceive the angelic and demonic ministries in a comparative and correct perspective. He thereupon recited the lines which he had memorised from his reading of the *Annual Register*. They ran as follows:

> Around the mouth of Hell a band
> Of fearful fiends for ever stand;
> Their bat-like bodies tense and stark,
> And on their heads the Beast's foul mark.
> These, should some Holy One draw near
> With store of love to give us cheer,
> All-spoiling Satan with quick shout
> Bids intercept and thrust him out.
> On ev'ry Seraph in the sky
> Keeps watch below a demon spy:
> Doth angel guard thee overhead?
> Two devils lurk beneath thy bed!
> So sleep not swordless, nor confide
> Too much to them of Michael's side;
> Lest, when the door of death is slammed,
> Thou find thyself among the damned.

Mr Tylethorpe had read in novels of people undergoing the sensation of seeming to witness their own speech and behaviour from a detached and exterior angle. Such a strange psychological experience was his at this moment. In the concluding part of his sermon the feeling was unmistakable: he listened to himself with growing surprise and disapproval. He misliked the lines that he quoted and, now that the hymn was being played over, he realised with a shock that (although to appear in the *Annual Register* they must have been written more than a century ago) they sounded nevertheless like a Satanic parody of the more modern verses they were about to sing. Others perhaps felt similarly; for the choir seemed half-hearted and in the middle of the last verse the blower let all the wind out of the organ. It was altogether a dismal performance and, helping after service to count the collection in the vestry, Mr Bugles was not quite his natural self.

"Them was true words as you uttered just now, sir; and as Solomon said, there be nought nastier than truth."

"But where did Solomon write that, Bugles?"

"I don't rightly know, sir, for I mind my grandfather's telling as how it were one of his unrecorded sayings. They were wonderful wise men, was Solomon and my grandfather."

As he walked down the churchyard path on his way back to the Rectory Mr Tylethorpe noted that such of his flock as he overtook, responded to his "good evening" with a more than usual deference. Or was it apprehension?

The self-surprise which his Michaelmas sermon awoke in the young Rector yielded before long to a growing interest in what had been its subject-matter. The fallen angels were seldom absent from his thoughts. Milton's *Paradise Lost* assumed a more goetic than poetic value for him, and he would sonorously declaim Tartarean passages from it in the pulpit.

There was only one conventicle of dissent in Tilchington, and this belonged to Mr Nehemiah Gattle, owner of a small market garden. It owned no allegiance or affiliation to any of the free churches, but had been started for the spiritual government of Mr Gattle by Mr Gattle for Mr Gattle. Nevertheless it had attracted the more or less regular attendance of twenty or so freelance religionists who, now that "Hell was preached proper at the church," deserted Mr Gattle for Mr Tylethorpe. In vain did the former expostulate that at "The Unsectarian Mission Hall" he had always preached an honest Protestant devil, and that the

Rector's demons were dirty Romish impostors whom Satan would scorn to recognise. The names of Samael and Asmodai fell like magic music on the bucolic ear and, as the Reverend Nigel's library on his new pet subject increased in quantity and diversity, a growing congregation would listen open-mouthed and enraptured to the legend of Lilith and other apocryphal narrations. A discourse on Isaiah xxxiv, 14, evoked an uneasy thrill; and another, upon the first six verses of Chapter ii of Job, was imaginative rather than exegetic. Even on Christmas Day the Rector focused his remarks on the astromancy of the Magi instead of on the sublime purpose of their journey: the sorcery of Simon Magus was somehow dragged into this untimely disquisition.

It was unfortunate for Mr Tylethorpe that there was no big house in Tilchington. The admonitions of a plain-speaking squire might have pulled him up at the brink whereon he now stood. As it was, the only person of any social position in the parish besides himself was a Mr Adrian Gribden, a letter from whom to an old college friend, written in January 1901, will throw light upon our story.

MY DEAR SMITH

I am so sorry you could not come for the New Year. There is little news to tell you, except that our worthy (?) incumbent intrigues me more and more. He is, believe me, surely and not slowly converting this countryside to a pseudo-mediaeval demonolatry. Those sermons I told you about in my last letter were in the nature of direct approaches to Manichaeism. Last Sunday he suc-ceeded in being even more corruptive

by prompting an undesirable reference to the Old Testament. You may remember that under a bequest of old Miss Hardham every seat in St Botolph's is provided with a copy of the Bible and Apocrypha. They are seldom opened, but there was an audible turning of leaves when Tylethorpe, preaching on the prodigal son, remarked that those of us who remembered the twenty-eighth chapter of the first book of Samuel, and especially the twenty-fourth verse, would realise that the return of the prodigal was not the only return associated in Holy Writ with a slaughter of the fatted calf. The result of this reference was of course that every one of his listeners, from old Bugles down to the newest joined choir-boy, was quickly reading how the witch of Endor brought up the shade of Samuel from the grave. This continual harping upon the sinister and occult cannot be good for anybody and, if I mistake not, Tylethorpe himself begins to show nervous strain. For instance, he keeps turning to look behind him in an unpleasantly odd and furtive fashion and has taken to preaching not from the front of the pulpit but with his back to the wall at its side; just as though he feared that somebody might look or lean over his shoulder. This attitude so impressed me on Sunday that I found myself half expecting to see him suddenly propelled forward by some invisible and unwelcome agency! But enough of this nonsense. Do try to get down for a week-end soon. They have put on a good afternoon train leaving town at 4.23, if you cannot manage the 12.57.

Yours sincerely,

A. GRIBDEN

The concluding sentences of this letter represent Mr Tylethorpe in transition from the first stage of his soul's malady to the second; from the active and enjoyed pursuance of a morbid interest to a passive and involuntary obsession by it. Before, however, we pass to the second phase, let us take a peep into his study towards the close of the first. He has again taken from his bookcase a volume of the *Annual Registers*, and it has again dropped from his hands during a perusal of the "Poetick Review." Asleep? No, hardly; because, as on a former occasion, he has memorised the lines he was reading. Can he find the page again? Bother it, no. Anyhow, he can jot them down from memory, and he does so. No authorship was subscribed, and he will send them tomorrow to the "literary inquiry column" of the *Commentator* for identification. Here are the lines:

Down the chasms of the night
Flashed a comet, purple-bright,
Prone upon whose lambent tail
Clung an angel deathly pale.
All the heaven cried for shame
When was read the angel's name,
The dear sad name of Zadyra.
Fairest of all angels he
Had gazed upon the crystal sea;
Saw his image mirrored there
And cried, 'I am than God more fair!'
Which hearing, Uriel
Flung him from sky to hell.
The coward moon
Sank seaward in a swoon:
But the brave sun,
Seeing what deed was done,
Rode forth to shine on other worlds afar,
To us becoming no more than a star,
Because of what was wrought on Zadyra.
Nor was the Earth unchanged:

Great shapes arose and ranged
Along the mountain sides; but no man
    saw
What these forms were: for there was
    light no more.

Neither the literary staff of the *Commentator* nor any of its readers proved able to trace the authorship of these lines, nor even to elucidate the name Zadyra.

4

THE SECOND, SOME might call it the hallucinative, stage of Mr Tylethorpe's decline started with his suspicion, which rapidly ripened into conviction, that he was not in sole occupancy of his new study. A succession of dreams, each of which came to him while resting in one of the big armchairs, left him in no doubt as to who was sharing it. So vivid was the first dream that he would have mistaken it for reality but for two things. The first was that, though he was seated facing the fire, his view of the room was as though he were standing with his back to it. The second was that the furniture had become entirely different from that which he had so recently chosen and installed. In his dream the window was closely shuttered but not curtained, and the floor was uncarpeted. Under the far wall was a long and deep chest, the size and shape of a church altar. On the door side of the room were two cases of shelves, the one filled with books and manuscripts and the other with what looked like laboratory equipment. At a large and untidy writing table in the bow window sat a black-habited figure, engaged apparently in limning some design on a pane of glass. Against one of the table legs leant a nine-light wooden window frame, whose shape and dimensions

Mr Tylethorpe at once recognised as those of the window in the south aisle of St Botolph's. On the table in front of the artist was propped a looking-glass into which he appeared to keep peering, and at his side lay a sketch in charcoal of an angel. As the dreamer surveyed this scene its central figure turned slowly from the table and looked him full in the face.

The features were both beautiful and familiar. They were in fact those of Lucifer in the church window. "So that was Phayne's self-portrait, was it?" ejaculated the Rector aloud, and thereby woke himself from the dream. Thenceforward, however, he lived in two rooms instead of one and, in both the dream room and the real, Nicolas Phayne lived with him. He thought and thought upon this sinister predecessor of his. Had anybody ever before so identified himself with the Evil One as to impersonate him in a self-portrait? It seemed a dangerously wicked thing to have done, and still more wicked was it to have perpetuated this impersonation in the window of a consecrated building confided to his charge. These and similar reflections probably caused the dream to repeat itself; for repeat itself it did, three or four times, and except in one small particular without variation. This one little change consisted in an appearance behind Phayne's back of visible disquiet in the air. It reminded the Rector of that peculiar crinkling of a view seen through waves of intense heat. He remembered in particular having once looked up at the sky above the open flue of a brick-kiln and seeing just such a rippling or disquiet interposed between him and the clouds. The only distinction was that the focus of disquiet behind Phayne was not amorphous but took roughly the shape of a figure, though without differentiation of limbs and parts. The last time that this dream was repeated Phayne, or rather the appearance of him, seemed for the first time to be conscious of something astir behind him. At first he made motions with his hands as though to brush away a gnat or moth, but finally he jerked round suddenly and saw. Mr Tylethorpe will never erase from his memory the horrible look that he then beheld. Surprise and fear were in it; but triumph also and never a trace of shame or remorse. After all, an offer had been made and accepted.

Mr Gribden's letter, reproduced some pages back, indicated the effect upon the Rector of this new factor in his dream. He began, in fact, to look for and to expect appearances of visible disquiet in the atmosphere of his own daily environment; and very soon imagination began to usurp the place of sensory observation. Miss Pristin quickly saw that something was going seriously wrong with her young master. First there was that senseless fuss that he made over a flaw in the glass of the garden door. If one looks through such a flaw naturally there must appear whorls or twists in the view seen through it; so where was the cause for him to break the window with his walking stick? Then came his sudden aversion to the pattern of the linoleum in the back passage. If he disliked a crinkly design, why had he himself chosen it barely five months ago? Well: she would have it rolled up and stored in the box room. Next occurred his complaints regarding the transparent shapes drawn by a night's frost on his bedroom window. Nothing could be done about those of course, except to keep the blinds drawn until they thawed out. Last and strangest whim of all, he forbade her ever again to wear on her bonnet her favourite big bow of black watered silk because (how could an educated man talk such nonsense?) "it all went alive and crinkly when she moved." This command Miss Pristin thought it wise to obey, but with the muttered reservation that she didn't hold with none such nasty fancies herself and hoped that somebody as she knew weren't forgetting to say his prayers regular.

"Forgetting?" Mr Tylethorpe rejoined, "There is no forgetting for me, Miss Pristin, no forgetting at all!"

The second dream that came to the Rector was not so distinct as the first; not because its verisimilitude was any the less, but because the scene presented was nocturnal and unilluminated except by a full moon shining through bare branches. At a block in front of a tree-trunk stood Nicolas Phayne with what looked like a black fowl fluttering in his left hand. With a downward sweep of his right arm there fell on the struggling animal an axe or other metal implement that glinted in the moonlight. A moment later he appeared to be dismembering the victim, and then to be doing something to it with water and a dull fire. So Phayne had sunk to this! Mr Tylethorpe's recent readings had taught him enough of goetic ritual for him to realise that he had visionally witnessed a preparation of Admixtures for the Evil Sacrifice. He dreaded, and yet yearned with a hideous impatience, to witness its consummation. This impatience waxed to a madness when, after the fashion of its predecessor, the immediate dream repeated itself a second and a third time. Nor was this psychological state without its inevitable effect: it prevented the sleep that would enable the coming of a final dream to resolve the horrid yearning in experience.

With the onset of this insomnia the

worsening of the Rector's condition could no longer be hid from his parishioners. For several Sundays past he had been reduced to reading a distinguished ecclesiastical dignitary's printed sermons, and Mr Gattle's errant sheep had promptly returned to the "unsectarian" fold. The Rector's reading of the liturgy had also become lifeless and perfunctory. "If t'poor parson," said Mr Bugles, "might be spoke of same as it might be one of my span'el pups, 'ud say as how he were sickening for distemper and p'raps 'll get through and may be not." Mr Gribden took a less charitable view and gave up going to church. At this juncture, also, the rectory servants decided to give notice but, fearing to face the master in his present mood and failing to obtain the mediation of Miss Pristin, they postponed any action on their resolve.

Whether Dr Marlock was professionally correct in coming to see the Rector on the summons of his housekeeper may be doubted, but that medical attention had become urgently necessary was obvious to everybody. The visit was not in itself a success, because the patient locked himself in his room and refused to see him. This, however, did not prevent Dr Marlock from leaving with Miss Pristin a small phial whose contents she undertook to pour into the after-dinner cup of coffee which Mr Tylethorpe, in spite of insomnia, still insisted on taking. It was indeed this surreptitious potion that induced sufficient sleep for the dreaming of his last dream.

Mr Tylethorpe had for some time given up trying to court sleep in his bed: having taken off his clothes and put on pyjamas and a dressing-gown he would return downstairs and settle himself down in an armchair before his study fire. The chair that he now chose was the one associated with his dreaming. On previous nights it had not been long before he was out of it again and pacing the room in an agony of sleeplessness. Tonight, however, thanks to the draught, he was sleeping soundly when Miss Pristin, who had taken upon herself a night's vigil at the doctor's request, looked in at half-past ten and again at eleven. The dream that now came to him was none the less terrible for being anticipated. The room appeared once more as in the first dream. Phayne, robed in a black preaching gown, stood before the altar-like chest, on which stood an array of sacred vessels (pyx, flagon, paten and chalice) and by their side a box and a bottle which the dreamer recognised as those seen in his previous dream. The postures and gestures of the figure before the chest made plain that a shameful travesty of Christianity's supreme rite was being enacted. Most of the figure's manipulations were mercifully half-hidden by the sleeves of the black gown, but suddenly the head tilted back and the upturned chalice showed for an instant in a foul climax of sacrilege. For long minutes thereafter the figure continued to stand in erect rigidity, but with successive tremors suggestive of extreme emotion or, it might be, physical pain. Then all at once the knees sagged, the body lunged, and there lay on the floor a black and motionless heap. The Rector started and awoke. The slight bleeding from his mouth was caused by his having bitten his lower lip.

The narration of this series of dreams will have taxed to breaking point the reader's capacity to bear with the obscene and macabre. Nevertheless there remains, and must be told, their immediate and still worse sequel. Madmen, as distinct from mental defectives, have been said to fall into three categories: those who think senselessly from senseless premises, those who think sensibly from senseless premises and those who think senselessly from sensible premises. The man who now shuddered in his night attire on his armchair belonged to the middle category. His ratiocination was quick, clear and concise; its basis in religion, philosophy and ethics was temporarily destroyed; it was rooted only in his present terror. He would never forget those dreams, even if they should not repeat themselves, which experience had taught him that they would. He could never rid himself of a consciousness of ghastly communion with the predecessor who had desecrated his priesthood in this room a century ago. Even if he should leave Tilchington, the spirit of Phayne, he felt certain, would accompany him, for were they not now fellow initiates in the Evil

Mysteries? He could certainly no longer continue in his Ministry, and when the reason for his abandoning it became known he would be shunned by all as insane or unclean. In short, life would not be livable; and a burden that cannot be borne must be laid down. He had heard suicides dubbed cowards by some and appraised as brave by others: but why prate of cowardice or bravery? It was just a natural process that a man should take his life when he can no longer live it. The necessary act would be short and simple. This dressing-gown cord was both strong and smooth; there was no fear of the noose that he had just made in it not pulling tight or of its breaking. Yes: he could just reach the curtain rod across the bow window by standing on the writing table, and the other end of the dressing-gown cord was soon made fast to it. Now the table must be pushed away, and a chair substituted: for he would never manage to kick from under him a heavy table. What an ugly scrooping sound its castors made! But not loud enough, luckily, to wake the servants. Here was a chair of just the right height. There now! All was ship-shape and ready.

Miss Pristin also observed that all was ready. Attracted by the scrooping of the table she had entered noiselessly and now stood behind Mr Tylethorpe. Her next action she has never explained, for she has never told it to anybody. Neither to Mr Tylethorpe nor to herself did an explanation seem necessary. It was an effect probably of the strain under which she had mustered resolve to enter the, to her, un-enterable room and of angry disgust at the scene on which she had intruded. Be this as it may, in a burst of violence and with all the strength at her command she first boxed the Rector's ears and then, as he turned in his astonishment, slapped his face. Worn to extreme weakness by insomnia and mental misery the wretched man passively dissolved in a flood of tears and, powerless to resist her seizure of his left forearm, allowed himself to be meekly led by her to his bedroom. There she locked him in and, having returned to the study, untied the dressing-gown cord from the curtain-rod and unknotted it. This was something which Dr Marlock need not see. Early next morning the physician found the patient still sleeping the sleep of exhaustion. In three days time he was strong enough to be taken by Dr Marlock and Miss Pristin in the midday train to Funtingham-on-Sea, where they left him in an efficient but not too fashionable Nursing Home.

5

CYRIL THUNDERSLEY, BY Divine Permission Bishop of Wintonbury, was entertaining a house-party at the Palace. No misogynist, but himself unmarried, he preferred male company and was ever a little apprehensive of lady guests. His present company at breakfast was such as he thoroughly enjoyed. There was old Dean Burnfell from Penchester who, still young at eighty, had more than half a century before been a minor canon at Wintonbury and had kept up his connections with the place ever since. On the host's other side sat the Colonial Bishop of Kongea, home on leave from his tropical see. Not yet forty, he still bustled and hustled with the momentum of youth. Next to him, and the only layman of the party, was Leslie Trueson, Fellow of St Peter's, Oxbridge, who was pursuing some historical researches in the palace library. The fifth person at the table was Mr Lemmet, the Bishop of Wintonbury's chaplain. Quiet and untalkative but invariably attentive, he had been well chosen for his present position.

"Until yesterday," remarked the Bishop of Wintonbury, "I imagined myself to be living in the twentieth century."

"You should never, my dear Cyril," rejoined Dean Burnfell, "pay too much attention to the almanacks. My life is nearing its close and it has been lived in many centuries. A man belongs to all the ages to which he is heir. I have found Plato more of a contemporary in many ways than most moderns. It is only births and deaths, not lives, that can be dated in Time's Register. Wordsworth, indeed, surmised that we come into the world trailing clouds of glory from an Ever Has Been. I don't know about that: but our religion assures us that we are destined for an Ever After and that we are in communion with departed saints."

"Quite so." Here the Bishop helped himself to a second sausage. "If it were a matter of communion with saints only, I should not have made my last remark. My reason for it was that, until faced yesterday by the fact, I would never have believed that a young priest of good family and excellent education, an athlete too, and a thoroughly manly fellow, whom I had specially selected for the best country living in the Diocesan gift, would have shamelessly taken to preaching sheer diabolism from his pulpit, and have ended by himself becoming demoniacally possessed; for such is my interpretation of the so-called breakdown that has necessitated his removal to a home for neurotics. It sounds like seventeenth or at latest eighteenth century history to me!"

"Yes," agreed Mr Trueson, "it is certainly reminiscent of the Tilchington Trouble, as it was called, a hundred years or more ago."

"What's that you say?"

"My dear Bishop, please don't look so startled! There is a manuscript account of the matter in your library. It was a perfectly straightforward case of what you have termed diabolism and it ended in the Rector's death."

"The man who has been received into a home for neurotics," said the Bishop impressively, "is none other than the present incumbent of Tilchington: young Tylethorpe."

"The deuce it is! Poor fellow, he may have found in his country cure something more than he bargained for. Lemmet, I wonder if you would be so good as to go across to the library, look up the index of manuscripts under T, and bring His

Lordship the paper docketed 'Tilchington Trouble.' If I remember right it's in one of the shelves under the oriel window."

No one spoke until Lemmet returned. Sausages are better enjoyed and more expeditiously consumed in silence. It was not, however, more than five minutes before the manuscript had been found and produced.

"You read it to us, Trueson," the Bishop requested, "as you are familiar with it."

"Certainly; I'll do my best, but it's a trifle illegible in parts. The docket bears a note over the initials P.V.R. (that would have been Bishop Ranwell) that he had found his perusal of the file so unedifying and distasteful that he had destroyed all its contents except this one paper which, in his opinion, contained all that was necessary to leave on record in the matter."

"I remember Ranwell," interpolated the Dean, "as a kind and gentle old man. He once bought up all the Jacks-in-the-Box in a toy shop here, because as a small boy he had been frightened by one!"

"Ah! did he so?" resumed Trueson. "That's what he may have intended to do in the present connection, if one may judge from what I shall now read to you. It is a letter dated the 3rd February, 1801, written by Archdeacon Howgall from his vicarage at Jedworth to Bishop Cumberley who, according to the panel in the Chapter House, was enthroned in 1794 and died in this palace in 1805. It was he who built the big block of stables and the extension to the palace wine-cellars. Now for the letter.

MY LORD BISHOP

The, I will not say lamented, death of Mr Phayne has relieved me of the pain and duty of adding to previous reports upon his malpractice and Your Lordship from the trouble and expense of processes necessary to his proposed deprivation.

In the final carriage of this matter I have obeyed throughout Your Lordship's ordinance for the avoidance of all scandal; whereto I have been mightily assisted by the phlegm and incuriosity of the local physician, Dr Lammerton. From the fact that all three Rectory servants were laid in bed with a sudden sharp colic after a meal of field puddocks picked in mistaking for mushrooms, whereof the dead man had also partaken, this learned doctor ascribed his death to none other cause and set his hand thereto in writing. The death chamber, as well as the body therein, were in fact unlooked upon until my arrival; but this not of intent or by discretion but by reason of general fear that there might be with the corpse such as were with him, as sundry assert, when alive.

On entering this room I locked the door behind me and half-closed the shutters against the window, so that I could see sufficiently within nor be seen from without. I will not distress Your Lordship with a tale of all that I there found, but will state enough to show that the cause of our true religion hath suffered nought by this death save an extreme good riddance. That here had been, to say least, a mockery of the Sacrament was plain shewn by paten and cup set out upon a table-chest. Each of which contained a separate stuff; the ingredients whereof appeared from an open handwritten book beside them. The prescriptions were of a rank poisonous sort and were without doubt the certain cause of death. Whether this Phayne was by law *felo de se* or no the physician has happily left us in no need to determine; and indeed I doubt it, for the name of the evil rite in his book was such as may have had him think that damnation of soul would have fetch't him immunity of body from poisons and such like harms. This with other ten or eleven books of like blasphemy and mischief I did make a fire of in the grate, and when the whole had waxed hot and consuming did pour thereon the substances from the sacred vessels. These latter, having found them to be not those used in the church but the property of the dead man, I placed with him in the coffin. For as none in Tilchington would so much as touch the body it fell to me to compose it therein, which I did without removal of any of the habiliments wherein I had found it.

The carriage of the coffin to the churchyard was done in a garden barrow, as
none would bear him on their shoulders,
and the grave had been dug in a portion
that was unconsecrate. None would
attend the burying; but the Sexton, his
two grown sons and myself did lower the
coffin without breaking thereof, although
it slipped from the forward ropes and fell
end on. The help of these good men was
on condition that I will say no prayers,
nor did I so but to offer thanksgiving
to Almighty God for deliverance of this
parish from Satan's curse.

In regard to the points of my second
and third letters, I caused the ash tree
and that which was below to be hewn
down and burned, as also the ivy bush
and grotto. I also loosed such animals
as remained. Conscience bids me dissent, but with humble deference, from

Your Lordship's view that exorcisation
is but a Romish vanity or superstition.
Nevertheless in obedience to Your
Lordship's wishes I abstained from all
motions there towards.

I have noted also Your Lordship's
judgment that if only parsons would do
more fox-hunting and less book-read-
ing this see of Wintonbury would be in
happier case. May I respectfully suggest
that exhortations to this end would
be more convincingly included in an
episcopal charge than in archidiaconal
admonitions?

Believe me to remain, My Lord Bishop,
Your most dutiful & obedient Servant,

T. HOWGALL
Archdeacon

"So you see, Bishop," added Mr Trueson, "that what has been worrying you is only the latest chapter in a serial story, 'The Tilchington Trouble'."

"It was a most reprehensible omission that should be remedied without delay," said the Bishop of Kongea.

"What was?"

"The omission to exorcise. We never dare run risks of that sort in Kongea. My sanctioned appendix to the Book of Common Prayer translated into Kongahili contains three occasional offices for the exorcisation of evil spirits. The first, relevant apparently to the rectory at Tilchington, is for their expulsion from buildings or places; the second for their ejection from infants and children; and the third for their removal from persons of riper years. All three Forms are in frequent use and of proved efficacy. We wouldn't be without them for anything.

Even the fauna of Kongea teaches us to appreciate the Petrine warning that our adversary the Devil walketh about as a roaring lion seeking whom he may devour."

The Bishop of Wintonbury walked to the window and for some minutes appeared wrapt in contemplation of a revolving cowl on one of his spare-room chimneys. He at length turned and addressed the Bishop of Kongea.

"You told me yesterday, Christopher, that you meant to spend a day in visiting Halmeston and Tilchington churches. I suppose from what you have just said that if you found yourself passing Tilchington Rectory you would feel it a moral obligation, even in the Rector's absence, to step inside and recite the office of which you have spoken?"

"I should certainly do so unless positively prevented. I have no English translation;

but, as I would be alone, its recital in Kongahili would be all right."

The Bishop of Wintonbury looked, as indeed he was, relieved. He did not wish to grant sanction as Diocesan to a ceremony that to his modern mind savoured of superstition. At the same time there were passages of scripture that could be quoted in justification of it, and many of the See's High Churchmen would certainly approve. Moreover, his personal scepticism in such matters had been severely strained that morning. He would not, therefore, expressly authorise the performance of the rite but, as his friend was minded to do it, he would not prevent it.

"Lemmet," he said, "I suggest you take a holiday from me tomorrow and accompany the Bishop of Kongea in the ten-thirty train to Tilchington. If you both carry sandwiches you can walk from there

to Halmeston and lunch on the common. That is to say, Christopher, if weather permits. It's no use doing such expeditions in the wet."

That night the wind rose to almost gale force and by morning had blown away the clouds and rain. The Bishop of Kongea and Mr Lemmet therefore set forth with the prospect of a bright if gusty day before them. All went according to plan for them except that Miss Pristin attended the service of exorcisation and, unable to follow the. Kongahili language, interspersed the rite at what appeared to her appropriate intervals with fervently ejaculated Amens. She had previously removed from their frames and now burnt in the kitchen fire, with full support from the Colonial Bishop, the two pictures that had hung on the walls. She also, after departure of the visitors and as her own particular contribution to a purification of the chamber, lit therein a sulphur candle of the sort used for medical disinfection.

The Bishop of Kongea was much interested in St Botolph's but one disappointment awaited him. The South aisle window, which was not protected by any wire grid on the outside, had been irreparably smashed that very morning, apparently only a few minutes before their entry into the church, by a small branch that had been snapped off one of the churchyard elms and hurled by the gale against the Western wall.

"I have always found exorcisation a very powerful rite!" the Colonial Bishop assured Mr Lemmet as they surveyed the debris.

6

A COMFORTABLE CONCLUSION to this history would have been that Nigel Tylethorpe after a full recovery returned to Tilchington and lived there happily ever afterward. That, however, was impossible. Even if his health had permitted a return, his *amour pro pre* would have forbidden it. But in point of fact his condition, both physical and mental, remained critical for more than a year: and then, on medical advice, he sailed on a world tour which occupied a further eighteen months. He had submitted his resignation of the incumbency to the Bishop within a fortnight of his first admission to the nursing home.

His successor, the Reverend Nathaniel Coltswood, brought with him to Tilchington a wife and seven children. He soon, of course, heard rumours about the room, but he made light of them. "We have made it the nursery," he declared, "and if Old Nick is minded to make off with a couple or so of the brats he's welcome to them. He can take his pick." In actual fact there has been no unrest or discomfort associated with the apartment since his induction.

The Reverend Sir Nigel Tylethorpe, Bart (for thus he returned from his long cruise owing to the unexpected death of Sir Sylvester, his first cousin) soon settled down in the old family seat of Battlewick Hall. On Sundays he assists the Vicar of Cubley-cum-Battlewick by reading Service at the small church within his park gates. He is still unmarried, but house parties at the Hall invariably declare his establishment to be the best managed in Westshire. The name of his housekeeper is, as you may have guessed, Roberta Pristin.

NDREW CALDECOTT (1884–1951) was a British colonial administrator and a writer of history and supernatural fiction.

ETH'S COMICS AND drawings have appeared in the *New York Times*, the *New Yorker*, the *Globe and Mail*, and countless other publications.

His latest graphic novel, *Clyde Fans*, won the prestigious Festival d'Angoulême's Prix Spécial du Jury.

He lives in Guelph, Ontario, with his wife, Tania, in an old house he has named "Inkwell's End."

Publisher's note: "A Room in a Rectory" was first published in *Not Exactly Ghosts* by Edward Arnold in 1947.

Library and Archives Canada Cataloguing in Publication

Title: A room in a rectory : a ghost story for Christmas / Andrew Caldecott ; designed and decorated by Seth.
Names: Caldecott, Andrew, Sir, 1884-1951, author. | Seth, 1962- illustrator.
Description: Series statement: Seth's Christmas ghost stories
Identifiers: Canadiana 2023047148X | ISBN 9781771965743 (softcover)
Subjects: LCGFT: Short stories. | LCGFT: Ghost stories.
Classification: LCC PR6005.A396 R66 2023 | DDC 823/.914—dc23

Readied for the press by Daniel Wells
Illustrated and designed by Seth
Copyedited by Ashley Van Elswyk
Typeset by Vanessa Stauffer

PRINTED AND BOUND IN CANADA